MW01098268

Blue's Clues & you!

5-MINUTE STORIES

Random House 🏠 New York

rhcbooks.com

ISBN 978-0-593-65229-9 (trade)

MANUFACTURED IN CHINA

10 9 8 7 6 5 4 3 2 1

CONTENTS

Rainy Day!

Illustrated by Susan Hall

Hi! It's me, Josh, and this is Blue. We're so glad you came over! We're always happy to have friends come and play on rainy days. There are so many great things we can do, even when it's raining!

I wonder what Blue wants to do on this rainy day.
We can play Blue's Clues to figure it out. Remember,
Blue's paw print will be on three clues. Blue's Clues!

To play Blue's Clues, we'll need our Handy Dandy Notebook! Sidetable Drawer made us a super-special Rainy Day Notebook. Thanks, Sidetable Drawer!

I really think I'm going to need your help to figure out what Blue wants to do on this rainy day.

Hey, we can watch the rain right through this window.

Do you see a paw print? Where?

The backyard! The backyard is our first clue.

Let's draw our first clue in our Handy Dandy Notebook! What could Blue want to do in the backyard on this rainy day? Hmm, I'm not sure. We need to find two more clues. Come on!

It's wet and windy, so I need my perfect rainy-day outfit!
I have an umbrella, rubber boots, and a rain jacket. They're all
waterproof! "Waterproof" means that water can't get inside to
make me all wet. My clothes and hair will stay nice and dry.
Oh, you see the second clue? Yeah, on my rain boots!

Let's draw rain boots in our Handy Dandy Notebook. What could Blue want to do on this rainy day in the backyard with rain boots? Hmm. We need to find one more clue!

Before we go out in the backyard, let's grab a treat from Mr. Salt and Mrs. Pepper for extra rainy-day energy. I'm going to have an apple. Blue wants some strawberries. What's your favorite snack?

Do you see the last clue?

Aha! It's on this splashing water!

Let's draw the splashing water in our Handy Dandy Notebook. We found all three clues! Now we're ready for our Thinking Chair.

Now that we're in our Thinking Chair, let's think. We need to figure out what Blue wants do on this rainy day. And our clues are . . .

. . . the backyard, rain boots, and splashing water.

Hmm, what could Blue want to do on this rainy day in the backyard, with rain boots and splashing water? Well, we can wear the rain boots on our feet when we go out into the backyard, but what could we do that makes splashing water?

Good thinking! Blue wants to go into the backyard and jump in puddles in her rain boots to make a splash! We just figured out Blue's Clues! Let's head into the backyard and get puddle-jumping with Blue. What a great way to play on a rainy day!

Now that we're outside, we can jump in little puddles, and we can jump in big ones, too. We can jump from one puddle to the next. Who can make the biggest splash?

Nice splashing, Blue!

Look, a rainbow! Let's name the colors of the rainbow. Red, orange, yellow, green, blue, and purple.

Thank you for coming over to play on this perfect rainy day!

Blue's Outdoor Playdate

Illustrated by Dave Aikins

Hi, It's me, Josh. I'm so glad you're here. It's a beautiful day, so Blue wants to do something outdoors with our friends—and that includes you! Ready? Great!

Blue isn't sure what to do outside. Should we go to Magenta's house?

Should we go to the backyard to play with Shovel and Pail?

Let's grab a snack with Mr. Salt and Mrs. Pepper and think about it. Yummy snacks always help me think.

Hmm. What should we do outside?

Blue has a great idea! We can have a picnic with some of our friends.

To tell our friends about the picnic, let's write invitations and give them to Mailbox to deliver. Thanks for your help, Mailbox! We can't wait to see you at our picnic later!

Next, we need some tasty treats to share with our friends at the picnic.

Oh, look! Mr. Salt and Mrs. Pepper made a cake and cupcakes to share with our friends. We can also take some delicious apples for a sweet and crunchy snack. Thank you, Mr. Salt and Mrs. Pepper!

Shovel and Pail always have the best ideas for playdates. Today they've brought something we can play with at the picnic. What is it?

Yeah! They brought a kite. Let's take turns holding the string and flying the kite in the wind. What a perfect way to play outdoors!

Purple Kangaroo and Orange Kitten are here.
They brought a big, bouncy ball. What game can
we play with a big, bouncy ball? We can play catch!
Let's play!

Magenta is here—yay! She and Blue are going to pick flowers for our picnic table.

It looks like they're finding new friends, too. Hello, green caterpillar! Hi, blue butterfly! Who's that on Magenta's nose? It's a red ladybug with tiny, black spots!

Whew, it's hot out here. Good thing I have my hat and sunscreen to protect me from the sun. It's important to wear sunscreen to keep our skin healthy and happy.

Now it's time to get the backyard ready for our picnic! Slippery Soap and Tickety Tock are helping me hang lanterns while Blue spreads the tablecloth. Paprika, Cinnamon, Sage, and Ginger are decorating the cupcakes. Nice teamwork, everyone!

How many cups do we need for lemonade? Let's count—one, two, three, four, five, six, seven, eight, nine, ten! We have ten cups of lemonade to share with our friends!

The decorations for our picnic look so
nice, and the flowers match Blue's tablecloth.
Everyone is enjoying the tasty treats. Blue
takes a bite of a big red apple. CRUNCH!

Magenta and Rainbow Puppy want to put on a show
for us to celebrate our wonderful picnic! Rainbow Puppy
will sing a song, and Magenta will play along on the
xylophone. They want to play a song about a spider
that's itsy . . . and bitsy. What song do you
think it is? Yeah, "Itsy Bitsy Spider"!
I love that song. Let's all sing along.

"*The itsy bitsy spider crawled up the waterspout.*
Down came the rain and washed the spider out.
Out came the sun and dried up all the rain,
and the itsy bitsy spider went up the spout again."

What a show!

This is such a perfect picnic! Thanks for coming!

Baking with Blue!

Illustrated by Dave Aikins

Hi, there! It's me, Josh! Welcome to Blue's Bakery, where everything smells sweet and delicious. Do you like sticky, crunchy cookies? Do you like sweet and tasty fruits? We can make all kinds of treats here. Will you help us?

Great! Come on in, baker friend!

Now, what should we bake today? Oh! Blue wants to make . . . bibingka! What a yummy idea! Bibingka is a tasty cake made of rice flour and coconut milk and is eaten around Christmastime in the Philippines. My *lola* makes the best bibingka!

This is my *lola*. *"Lola"* means "grandma" in the Philippines. That's where my family is from! I miss my *lola,* so I have her picture on the wall to remind me of her.

Baking yummy treats from the Philippines always reminds me of her, too. I always loved it when she let me help her cook delicious treats, but her bibingka was my favorite. It's *masarap*! *"Masarap"* is how we say "delicious" in the Philippines. There are so many *masarap* foods from the Philippines!

Who should we bake this bibingka for, Blue?

Oh! Let's play Blue's Clues to find out who gets to enjoy the bibingka with us. Will you help?

Great! Let's keep an eye out for clues while we start making this bibingka.

Do you see a clue? Yeah, it's on this heart! Let's put this first clue in our Handy Dandy Notebook!

Hmm, what could this heart mean? Sometimes a heart means "love." Maybe we're baking this bibingka to share with someone we love! We should keep looking for more Blue's Clues to figure this out.

Now that we've put all our ingredients in the bowl, it is time to mix everything together. What can Blue use to mix? Yeah! Blue can use a spoon!

Mix, mix, mix! Great job, Blue!

It's almost ready to go in the oven, but first we need to add . . . the pineapple!

Pineapple is the secret ingredient in my *lola*'s bibingka recipe. That's how you know it's her special creation.

I love sweet and juicy pineapple. There are so many fruits that are *masarap*—apples, pears, oranges . . . What's your favorite? Yum! I like those, too.

My *lola*'s recipe says that we need four slices of pineapple for the bibingka. How many do we have here?

One, two, three, four, five, six, seven! We have more than enough for our bibingka! And we can make even more pineapple treats for our friends after our cake is done.

Now our bibingka is ready for the oven.
Thanks for helping us make my *lola*'s special recipe.
Come on, let's go to the Living Room while we wait
for our bibingka cake to be ready.

Look! It's another clue . . . on these glasses! Let's draw the glasses in our Handy Dandy Notebook.

We have two clues—a heart and glasses! Who gets to enjoy the bibingka with us? I think we need to find the last clue! Let's find it before our bibingka cake is done!

Oh, the house smells sweet! Our bibingka is almost ready. I can't wait! But we still don't know who we are baking this bibingka for. Where is that last clue?

Do you see a paw print? Yeah, it's outside, on that blue-striped scarf on the clothesline! We have all three clues! You know what that means? It's time for our Thinking Chair!

Let's think. We have a heart for love, glasses, and a blue-striped scarf. Hmm, someone I love with glasses and a scarf—who could it be?

My *lola*! Yes! We can enjoy this bibingka cake with my *lola*! She'll love it!

We just figured out Blue's Clues—because we're really smart!

I hear a knock on the door! Who could that be?

It's my *lola*! Welcome to Blue's Bakery. I'm so
excited that you're here! She came all the way from the
Philippines. That's so far! She must have really missed
me. I missed you, too, Lola. I love you! That's why we
made the bibingka cake to share with you!

Here's a slice for me, a slice for Lola, a slice for Blue . . . and a slice for YOU!

Lola thinks the bibingka is *masarap*! I learned from the best! Thank you, Lola! And thank YOU for all your help! What a delicious day!

Blue Loves You!

Illustrated by Steph Lew

Happy Love Day! It's really busy in our house today because we are getting ready for our Love Day party . . . and you're invited. Come on in!

Love Day is when we celebrate everyone we love. To show them our love, we give them cards we made. I love Blue . . . and she loves me, too! We made each other cards. Who do you love? You should tell them . . . or show them with a card! You can also show them with a big hug!

Blue is making a special surprise for our Love Day party. I wonder what it is. Hey, let's play Blue's Clues to figure it out! Remember, Blue's paw print will be on the clues. Blue's Clues! We need to find each paw print and put the clues in our Handy Dandy Notebook!

Let's go find some clues.

I just can't wait for the Love Day party. It's so awesome getting Love Day cards. Have you ever made a card? All you need are paper and crayons. You can also decorate a card with stickers and glitter. I made Love Day cards right here at the table.

Yeah, I used glue. Oh, you see a clue? Where?

Paper! That's our first clue! Let's put it in our Handy Dandy Notebook. Hmm, so what surprise could Blue be making with paper? Maybe! But we need to find more clues!

What a gorgeous day! The sun is shining, and the sky is clear, so we're going to have our Love Day party out in the backyard. Our friends have been hanging up decorations. Look how pretty they've made the yard look. How many hearts do you see?

One, two, three!

And how many balloons do you see?

One, two, three, four, five, six, seven, eight!

Nice counting!

Slippery Soap is making Love Day cards, too. He made
cards for Sidetable Drawer, Shovel, and Pail. In each
card, he drew what he loves about his friends. I'm sure
Slippery will get plenty of Love Day cards, too.
Do you see another clue? Where? On the crayon!

Crayons are our second clue! Let's put it in our Handy Dandy Notebook. So, what could Blue be making for Love Day with paper and crayons? I have so many ideas! I think we need to find our last clue to be sure.

Do you hear that? It's Mail Time! Happy Love Day, Mailbox! I *love* how you sing about Mail Time. See you later at the party.

Mailbox has a Love Day card for us! Wow, I feel so loved. Don't you, Blue?

It's almost time for the party. But where is Blue? Let's find her. Hey, do you see a paw print? Oh, on those pipe cleaners. That's our third clue! Let's draw them in our Handy Dandy Notebook. We have all three clues! You know what that means? We're ready to sit in our Thinking Chair!

Let's think! We need to figure out what Blue is making for Love Day. Our clues are paper, crayons, and pipe cleaners. Hmmm . . . what could Blue be making?

What if Blue used the crayons to draw pictures on the paper, and then used the pipe cleaners to tie all the pages together. What would that be?

A book! Yeah, Blue made a Love Day book! She drew on paper with crayons and put the pages together with pipe cleaners to make a Love Day book for us. Thank you, Blue! I *love* it, and I love YOU!

And I really love it when we figure out Blue's Clues . . . together!

Thank you for all your help today. Now we can have our Love Day party. What a great way to spend the day. We sure love having a friend like you.
Happy Love Day!

THE RAINBOW SHOW!

Illustrated by Dave Aikins

Hi! It's me, Josh! Blue and I are so happy you're here. Today we are celebrating two of our favorite things: friends and rainbows!

The colors of the rainbow are different, but they come together in a beautiful way. Just like our friends! We are going to celebrate our rainbow of friends with a Rainbow Show. Will you help us get ready for it? Great!

Blue and Magenta are best friends. Blue has blue fur, and Magenta has magenta fur. They look different, but they both like to play outside, use their imagination, and spend time together.

Blue and Magenta are happy whenever they spend time together. They are planning something special for the show today!

Magenta wears glasses, and Purple Kangaroo doesn't wear glasses. They love to read together! Their favorite stories all start with "Once upon a time . . ."

They want to act out one of the stories in their book at the Rainbow Show. I wonder which one they will choose. Do you have a favorite story?

Shovel and Pail are brother and sister. They are different shapes, and they like to do different things. Shovel likes to dig in the dirt and sand, while Pail likes to build sandcastles.

But they have a lot in common, too. They both like to wear silly hats, tell jokes, play in the backyard, and go to the beach. When they work together, they make a great team!

Shovel and Pail are in charge of the balloon decorations for the Rainbow Show. They want to bring balloons in every color of the rainbow!

Sidetable Drawer is big, and Tickety Tock is small. Tickety likes to count, and Sidetable Drawer likes to sing.

Even though Sidetable and Tickety look very different and like different things, they are good friends.

They both love the nursery rhyme "Hickory Dickory Dock" because it has numbers, and they can sing it together! They're going to sing it later at the Rainbow Show. I can't wait!

Sage and Ginger are younger than Paprika and Cinnamon. Sage and Ginger like to take baths in the sink, while Paprika and Cinnamon like to build things with objects they find around the kitchen.

They are all part of the same family. Big or small, they all love to have fun together during family playtime.
  Where do you think they're all racing off to in their vegetable cars? It looks like fun! Hopefully they'll race into the Rainbow Show later.

Orange Kitten has pointy ears, and Blue has floppy ears. Their ears are different sizes and shapes, but they both love to use them to listen to music!

Blue and Orange Kitten will do a dance while
I play the guitar at the Rainbow Show. What song
should we sing? Great idea!
   Will you dance with us at the Rainbow Show?
Hooray!

This is a picture of me and my grandmother. I call her my *lola*. She grew up far away from here, in the Philippines. I grew up here.

Even though we're from different places, we're still a family! We like to talk to each other on the phone and send each other letters.

We are happy when we can spend time together.
She makes the best bibingka cake using coconut
and rice flour!

Blue and I will send Lola a video of the concert
so she can watch it, too.

Blue and Magenta are painting a picture of all our friends to display at the Rainbow Show! That's their surprise! They are mixing blue, red, and yellow paints together to make all the colors of the rainbow.

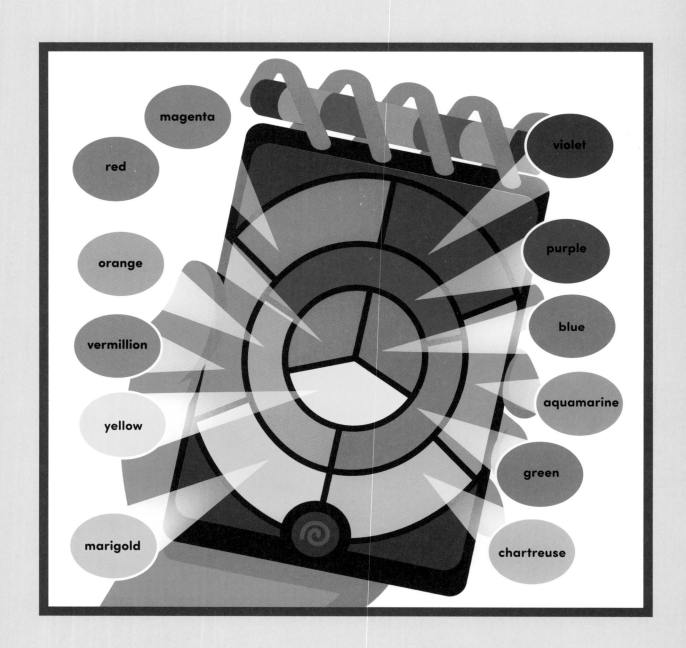

Look at how colorful their portrait is! Nice job, Blue and Magenta!

RAINBOW SHOW

The things that make us different make us special, too. Our differences bring us together! Just like the colors of the rainbow, when we come together, we can make something beautiful.

Now it's time for our Rainbow Show! Some friends are singing. Others are dancing. I'm playing music. But together, we make one amazing show!

I'm so glad we're all here, and I'm extra glad that YOU are here with us. Let's celebrate our differences—today and every day!

Farm Friends!

Illustrated by Dave Aikins

Hi there! I'm Josh. It's a beautiful day, so Blue and I skidooed to the farm! We love to visit the farm to see our animal friends. We like the pigs, cows, and chickens. Our friend Farmer Goat asked us to check in on everyone on the farm for her. Will you help us? Great!

Blue is excited to see her farm animal friends. But what else does Blue want to do on the farm? Will you play Blue's Clues with me to figure out what Blue wants to do? Great!

Our first stop at the farm is at this great big pasture. I see cows and sheep munching on the grass. Hi, cows! Hi, sheep! Cows say *moo*. Let's *moo* like a cow! *Mooooo!* Nice mooing! Sheep say *baa*. Let's *baa* like a sheep! Baaaa! The sheep are *baaing,* too!

Look at the baby farm animals. A baby cow is called a calf, and a baby sheep is called a lamb. I call them both "soooo cute!"

Wait, do you see a paw print? Yeah, on the grass.

Grass is our first clue.
Let's put it in our Handy
Dandy Notebook!

It's such a beautiful day on the farm. The sun is shining, and the fields are green. Let's look for more clues in the old red barn. This is where Farmer Goat keeps tools and machines. It's also where some of our farm friends live.

Before we go into the barn, let's say hello to this pig and little piglet! Pigs say *oink, oink*. Say *oink, oink* to the pigs!

Splish, splash, sploosh. The pigs are rolling in the mud. That helps them cool down on sunny days like this. Rolling in the mud looks like fun . . . but maybe it's a little too messy for us.

There are more farm friends inside the barn! Hello, mama horse! Hello, little pony! Horses can run very fast. When they meet a friend, they say *neigh*. Will you say *neigh* to our four-legged friends?

Hey! That looks like some tasty hay you're eating!

And what's that? A clue!

Oh! There's a paw print on that blanket! Let's draw it in our Handy Dandy Notebook.

So we have two clues: grass and a blanket. What could Blue want to do on the farm with grass and a blanket? Hmm. We'd better find that last clue!

Here's the chicken coop. I don't see a clue in here, but I do see a whole bunch of friends! Blue wants to say hi to the whole chicken family. Look them flapping their feathery wings! Can you wave your arms like flapping wings to say hi to the chickens?

The mother hen says *cluck, cluck*. The chicks say *peep, peep*.
What does the rooster say? Cock-a-doodle-doo!

Do you know what's near the chicken coop? The pond where other feathered farm friends live!

I see a duck and a little duckling swimming around. They quack a hello at us! *Quack, quack* to you, too, little ducks!

Do you see another clue?

Yeah! The clue is next to the duck pond on that
basket full of food! We have all three clues. Time for the
Thinking. . . . Hmm. We don't have our Thinking Chair
here on the farm. What should we do? I know, let's sit on
the Thinking Tractor!

Let's think. What could Blue want to do at the farm with grass, a blanket, and a basket full of food?

What do you think Blue wants to do?
A picnic! Yeah, Blue wants to have a picnic
with her farm friends! We just figured out Blue's
Clues! What a great day for a picnic on the farm!

I'm so glad that all our new friends came to the picnic! *Farm*-tastic! Let's sing a song with our farm friends!

"Old MacDonald had a farm, E-I-E-I-O!
And on his farm, he had a cow,
 E-I-E-I-O!
With a moo-moo here and a moo-
 moo there,
Here a moo, there a moo,
 everywhere a moo-moo,
Old MacDonald had a farm,
 E-I-E-I-O!"

Thank YOU for helping me figure out Blue's Clues. You sure are smart! See you soon!

Blue's Winter Day!

Illustrated by Dave Aikins

Hi there! It's me, Josh! I'm so glad you came over to play with us on this snowy day. My favorite thing to do on a snowy day is run in the snow. Oh, no, wait—my favorite, favorite thing is cozying up inside with a cup of delicious hot chocolate. Hmm, actually—my favorite, favorite, *favorite* thing is ice-skating!

I just can't decide—there are so many great ways to spend a snow day! What do you want to do, Blue?

What a great idea! We can play Blue's Clues to find out what Blue wants to do on this snowy day! Will you help me? Great! Remember, we need to find all three clues and put them in our Handy Dandy Notebook. Let's go!

First stop, the kitchen! I bet Mr. Salt and Mrs. Pepper are cooking up a warm, delicious snack on this cold, snowy day!
You see a clue already? Where?

A carrot! Let's draw it in our Handy Dandy Notebook. What could Blue want to do on a snowy day with a carrot? Carrots are yummy. Do you think Blue wants to eat a carrot? Hmm. We'd better find our other two clues.

Look! Shovel and Pail are outside enjoying the snow. They made four snowballs.

Which one is the biggest snowball? Which is the smallest? Do you see two snowballs that are the same size?

Super snowball-sizing!

Let's keep looking for clues on this snowy day. Maybe there's something in the Living Room. . . .

Hmm. There's a top hat in the middle of the Living Room. That's strange!

Oh! There's a paw print on the hat. That means it's our
second clue. Let's put it in our Handy Dandy Notebook.
So our first two clues are a carrot and a top hat.
Interesting. . . . I think we'd better find the last clue.

It's Mail Time! Even in the snow, Mailbox always delivers the mail. Look! We got an amazing paper snowflake chain in our letter. I love making snowflake chains, and I love it even more when friends share their beautiful art with us. Thanks, Mailbox!

This is such a lovely snowflake chain. We should show it off by hanging it over the window. It's the perfect decoration for this snowy winter day.

What's that? You see another clue? Where?

There's a paw print on the snow. Let's draw snow in our Handy Dandy Notebook. Hey, it's the third clue! You know what that means! It's time for the Thinking Chair!

Hmm . . . so what could Blue want to do on this Snowy Day with a carrot, a hat, and snow? Blue wants to build a snowman! You are so smart!

We just figured out Blue's Clues! Now let's go make that snowman. It's frosty and windy out. We'd better bundle up. I've got my jacket, snow boots, hat, mittens, scarf, and earmuffs so I'll be nice and warm. Blue does, too. Ready for the snow?

Our friends Shovel, Pail, Mr. Salt, Mrs. Pepper, and Mailbox want to join us. Hey, we can use the snowballs Shovel and Pail were making earlier, too!

To build a snowman, you put a big snowball on the bottom, a medium snowball on top of that, and a little snowball on the very top. We use rocks to make a face and some buttons on the body, sticks for arms, and we use the carrot for a nose. For the finishing touch, let's put the top hat on top.

Ta-da! What a beautiful snowman. And what a great winter day! Thanks for joining us!

BLUE'S BUSY DAY!

Illustrated by Dave Aikins

Hi there! I'm Josh. Have you seen my friend, Blue?

There she is! Blue and I are happy you're here to spend the day with us. We have a busy day ahead! Do you want to join us? Great, let's get going!

First, let's think about we need to do on this busy day.
Whenever I need to think, I sit in our . . . Thinking Chair!

Wow, look at the rain outside. I'm glad Mailbox has a raincoat and hat to keep him dry!

I hope the rain stops soon. Until then, we can keep busy inside!

While we wait for the sun to come out, we can use our imagination to have fun with our friends right here. Let's use our imagination to turn the house into . . . Superheroville! We are all pretending to be superheroes. I'm Song Man. With my friends Super Blue, Clock Girl, and Super Soap, we are the Thinking Squad. You can be part of our Thinking Squad, too! What is your superhero name ? Nice!

For our superhero good deed, we need to help Periwinkle find his sparkly superhero cape! Do you see it?

That was super fun—and it made me super hungry! Let's go get a tasty snack from Mr. Salt and Mrs. Pepper!

Mrs. Pepper needs us to watch the twins while she gets our snack! No problem! Baby Sage and Baby Ginger are so cute!

Oh, look! It stopped raining, and the sun is out! Now there is a beautiful rainbow and I can also see a few clouds.

Blue and I love to look up and find shapes in the clouds. What shapes do you see?

Next, Blue wants to go to the Present Store to get a present for Magenta. This is such a busy day!

Blue thinks Magenta would like something that's soft, cuddly, and purple.

Which toy should Blue get for Magenta?

Yeah! The soft, cuddly, purple bear!

Now Blue has led us to the park! Our friends are here for a party, including Magenta! Magenta loves the present Blue gave her. Thanks for your help!

What a great day in the park! Slippery Soap is on a skateboard. Purple Kangaroo is jumping rope. I have a ball. There's so much we can do to have fun and stay busy!

Next, Blue and I
skidoo to the farm!
We're going to help
feed the animals.

The cows are eating
grass. The horses and
sheep are eating hay.
The pigs are eating feed
from a trough.

Farmer Goat needs help bringing the fruits and vegetables from the farm to sell at the market. We're having a busy day, but we're never too busy to help our friends! Let's help Farmer Goat with all her delicious fruits and vegetables. What fruits and vegetables do you like? Me too!

Blue wants to keep busy with one more skidoo! Where to, Blue?

Here we are in outer space with the sun and all the planets. Pluto is so small that it's called a dwarf planet. It's even smaller than our moon! Jupiter is the biggest planet! But my favorite is our home—Planet Earth! What's your favorite planet?

Along with the planets, we can
see stars. A group of stars is called a
constellation. Hmm . . . I think that
constellation looks a lot like someone
we know.

131

After our big, busy day, Blue is ready to relax in a bubbly bubble bath. What else does she need to do to get ready for bed at the end of a busy day? Slippery Soap knows!

After her bath, Blue needs to brush and floss her teeth, brush her hair, use the potty, wash her hands, and wash her face before she goes to bed.

Blue and I are reading one of our favorite bedtime books, *Good Night, Bird*. It always makes us feel sleepy.

After story time, we'll sing a good-night song. Then it's off to bed. We had such a fun, busy day. We are so glad you could spend it with us!

What do you think Blue will
dream about tonight?
Sweet dreams, Blue!

Good Night, Blue!

Illustrated by Dave Aikins

Hi it's me, Josh! You're just in time to watch the sun set with us! As the sun goes down, the sky gets darker until it's nighttime. I love sunsets. The sky gets so colorful with reds and yellows and oranges until it's finally black.

Now that it's dark out, it's time for our Pajama Party! That's when we all get together in our pajamas and have fun until bedtime! I'm wearing my favorite, fluffiest pajamas. I hope you're nice and cozy, too!

Our friends are coming over for our Pajama Party. Blue wants to do something extra special with them. Oh! We can play a nighttime game of Blue's Clues to figure out what Blue wants to do at the Pajama Party. Will you help me find all three clues? Great!

Looking for paw prints is a perfect Pajama Party game. Let's find the clues before we start yawning!

Do you see the first clue? Where?

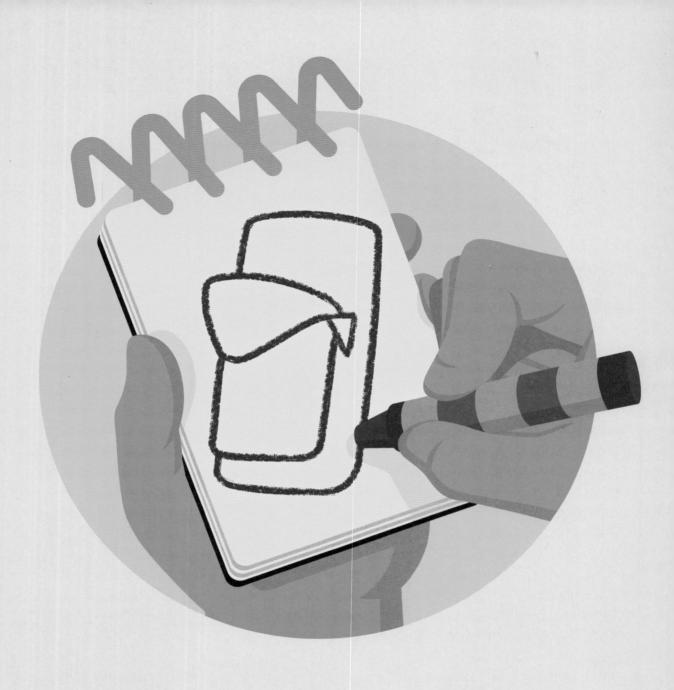

It's a sleeping bag! It's purple with pink polka dots on it, and it looks super cozy! Let's draw it in our Handy Dandy Notebook.

What could Blue want to do at the Pajama Party with a sleeping bag? We need two more clues!

Oooooh. I hear our friends outside. Let's go!

Hi, Shovel! Hi, Pail!

Look, Shovel and Pail made a new friend. Who? *Hoo? Hoo?*

It's an owl! Owls are birds with big eyes for seeing really well at night. They stay awake at night and sleep during the day!

Enjoy the night, Owl! It's been a real hoot. Shovel and Pail are going to get ready for the Pajama Party, and we need to get back to looking for clues!

I'm starting to get a little sleepy. The stars and moon are out already—I love how they shine and twinkle. Hey, something else is shining, too . . . is that our second clue?

Yeah! Our second clue is a lamp. What could Blue want to do with a sleeping bag and a lamp? I think we'd better find our last clue.

It's Mail Time . . . at night! Hi, Mailbox! I like your Pajama Party sleeping cap.

We just got a package! I wonder who it's from?

Ahh, it's from my *lola*! My grandma sent me a cozy blanket for nighttime. Perfect for a Pajama Party at night!

Hey . . . why does it get dark at night?

Great idea, Blue! We can skidoo into space to find out why it gets dark at night. Let's wear our blankets as capes, so we can be . . . pajama-nauts! That's like an astronaut, but in our pajamas.

Let's skidoo to space! Blue skidoo—we can, too!

We live on planet Earth, and it's always spinning. When our place on Earth spins *away* from the sun, it gets dark. We call that nighttime. When it faces *toward* the sun, it gets light. We call that daytime. Right now, our house is facing away from the sun, so it's dark and nighttime!

What an *out-of-this-world* discovery! Whoa, I'm getting to be one sleepy pajama-naut! Let's get back home to Earth and find our last clue.

We're back from our Outer Space Skidoo!
Whoo-hoo! And what's that? You see a clue?

It's a book! Let's draw it in our Handy Dandy Notebook! That's our third clue, and you know what that means? We're ready to sit in our Thinking Chair!

Let's think! We're trying to figure out what Blue wants to do at our Pajama Party with a sleeping bag, a lamp, and a book. Hmm . . . a sleeping bag is cozy and a lamp gives off light . . . to read a book . . .

Aha! Blue wants to get cozy in her sleeping bag and read a book by the light of the lamp. We just figured out Blue's Clues!

All our friends are here for the pajama party. We've all snuggled up in our sleeping bags to read *Good Night, Bird.*

What a good book. Now, before we go to sleep, let's sing one last song. Join in if you know it!

"Twinkle, twinkle little star, how I wonder what you are.
Up above the world so high, like a diamond in the sky.
Twinkle, twinkle little star, how I wonder what you are."

Thanks for coming to our Pajama Party and helping to figure Blue's Clues. Good night!